This book belongs to

Joseph

Abby Lily trenton

This is the story of Three Billy Goats Gruff,

You can read it yourself – it's not very tough.

Why not have a try, if you're brave enough!

One thing more. Can you guess what?

On every page there's worm to spot!

Three Billy Goats Gruff

Nick and Claire Page

Illustrations by Katie Saunders

make
believe
ideas

In the valley, by a river,
Lived three happy billy goats.
One was small: **Little Will**,
with a bell around his throat.
One was tall: **Brother Bill**,
with a big and shaggy coat.
One was HUGE: **Rough Tough Gruff**.
He could turn you into fluff!

On the mountain, by a bridge,
Lived a nasty troll called Sid.
He had eyes – big as pies,
Ears like two big saucepan lids!
Yellow teeth, wrinkly throat,
And his favourite food was goat!

In the valley, one fine day,
There was not much grass around.
"Time to go," said Little Will.
"Let's climb up to higher ground.
Cross the bridge, to the pass
Where there's loads of lovely grass!"

So the three goats trotted off
To the bridge up by the pass.
"I'll go first," said Little Will.
"Look at all that lovely grass."
Trip-trap-trip! As he ran,
Sid the Troll jumped out and sang...

9

"Don't want chicken,
Don't want lamb,
Don't want bacon,
Don't want ham.
Don't want beef,
Or veal, or pork.
Want some goat
Upon my fork!"

Keep off

Little Will sweetly smiled,
And he gave a little bleat.
"Don't have me for your tea;
I am not much good to eat.
But if goat is your prize,
Why not try some Goat Surprise?"

"Goat Surprise?" said the troll.
"Oooh, that sounds completely yummy!"
"Just you wait," said Little Will,
"And you'll have some in your tummy.
My big bro' can tell you more
About this meal so scrummy.
Let me through, if you will."
And he crossed onto the hill.

Brother Bill came along
With his great, big, shaggy coat.
And up and onto the bridge,
Went this brave, strong billy goat.
Trip-trap-trip! As he ran,
Sid the Troll jumped out and sang...

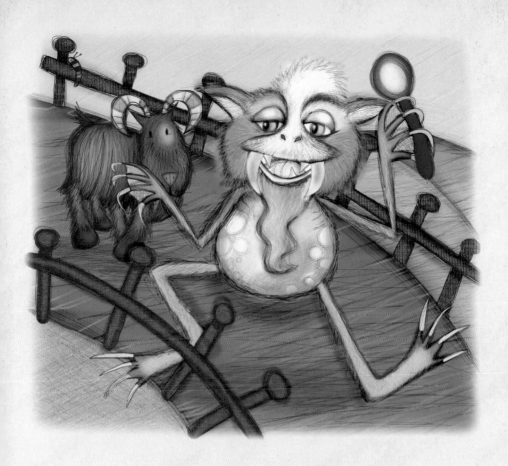

"Don't want apples,
Don't want cherries,
Don't want peaches,
Don't want berries.
Don't want plums
Or figs or prunes.
Want some goat
Upon my spoon!"

Brother Bill calmly stood
And he gave a little baa.
"Don't have me for your tea;
Eating me won't get you far.
But to fill your insides
You should try some Goat Surprise."

"Goat Surprise?" said the troll.
"Ooooh! Sounds absolutely great!"
"In a mo'," said Brother Bill,
"You will have some on your plate!
My big brother will be here –
All you have to do is wait.
Let me through, let me pass."
And he went to eat some grass.

Rough Tough Gruff soon appeared,
And up to the bridge he sped,
He was huge, he was fierce,
With great horns upon his head.
**Trip-trap-trip! As he ran,
Sid the Troll jumped
out and sang...**

"Don't want lettuce,
Don't want beans,
Don't want cabbage,
Don't want greens,
Don't want carrots,
Peas or shallots!
Want some goat
here in my pot!"

Rough Tough Gruff just stood still,
And he said to Sid the Troll,
"If it's goat that you want,
You can put me in your bowl.
Pick on someone your own size!
Here's my special Goat Surprise!"

"Goat Surprise?" cried the troll.
"Oooooh, it's come my way at last!"
Then he saw Rough Tough Gruff
Charging straight towards him, fast!
Sid felt sick, when a kick
Hit him like a mighty blast.

Rough Tough Gruff put Sid in plaster,
Then he went to munch some pasture.

Those three goats set up home,
On that green and grassy hill,
With a munch they had their lunch,
Rough Tough Gruff and Bill and Will.
Sid the Troll disappeared;
All his friends said he was ill.
From then on, you will note,
He couldn't stand the taste of goat.

Keep off.

25

Ready to tell

Oh no! Some of the pictures from this story have been mixed up! Can you retell the story and point to each picture in the correct order?

27

Picture dictionary

Encourage your child to read these harder words from the story and gradually develop their basic vocabulary.

bridge

dinner

goat

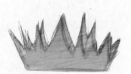

grass

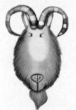

horns

mountain

river

troll

worm

Key words

Here are some key words used in context. Help your child to use other words from the border in simple sentences.

The goats **like** grass.

Bill stood **on** the bridge.

Sid had **big** teeth.

"Goat is **my** favourite dinner!"

Gruff charged **at** him.

Grow a grassy meadow

The billy goats wanted to get up to the good grass on the green meadow. Here's how to grow a beautiful "meadow" that you can enjoy eating.

You will need

a new face cloth, or about ten sheets of kitchen towel
• a large plate or plastic tray • mustard and cress seeds
• scissors • a spoon

What to do

1 Put the face cloth, or pile the sheets of kitchen towel, on the plate or tray. Soak the cloth or paper by spooning cold water onto it.

2 Sprinkle mustard and cress seeds over the damp cloth or paper.

3 Put the plate or tray on a sunny windowsill.

4 Sprinkle with water each day so the paper doesn't dry out. At the same time you can see if your seeds are growing tiny shoots or sprouting green leaves.

5 After a few days your "meadow" will be covered in green mustard and cress "grass" that's ready to harvest. Use the scissors to cut off as much as you need.
Mustard and cress taste very good in egg sandwiches. You could probably even eat it with roast goat – but don't tell Sid the Troll!